SUPERHERO
INSTRUCTION MANUAL

ISBN 978-1-338-21756-8

Text copyright © 2016 by Kristy Dempsey. Cover art and interior illustrations copyright © 2016 by Mark Fearing. All rights reserved. Published by Scholastic Inc., 557 Broadway, New York, NY 10012, by arrangement with Alfred A. Knopf, an imprint of Random House Children's Books, a division of Penguin Random House LLC. SCHOLASTIC and associated logos are trademarks and/or registered trademarks of Scholastic Inc.

12 11 10 9 8 7 6 5 4 3 2 1   17 18 19 20 21 22

Printed in the U.S.A.   40

First Scholastic printing, September 2017

The illustrations in this book were created using pencil and digital color.

For my nephews:
Drew, Mac, Mills, and Zae,
who are super
without even trying.
—K.D.

For Jace and Lena,
two super kids!
—M.F.

SUPERHERO
INSTRUCTION MANUAL

by **Kristy Dempsey**

illustrated by **Mark Fearing**

SCHOLASTIC INC.

Do you have what it takes to be a hero and **save the world**? Are your muscles made of **elastic**? Are your bones made of **steel**?

Can you **soar through the air** with a single leap?

Never fear. Our one-of-a-kind

SUPERHERO Instruction Manual

will turn you super in

seven easy steps.

STEP 1: CHOOSE A SUPER NAME

Need help? Combine your favorite color
with your favorite animal. Be the Green Tiger.
Or the Pink Python.
With two little words,
you even *sound* super!

STEP 2: PICK A PARTNER

Holy donut, hero! You need a sidekick!
Choose wisely. Remember, your sidekick
will look up to you and hope
to become a hero, too.

STEP 3: CRAFT A SUPER DISGUISE

Unitard.

POW!

Mask.

BAM!

Are you feeling super yet?*

*Legal notice: As a safety precaution, the *Superhero Instruction Manual* strongly recommends a well-fitting helmet as part of your superhero ensemble. The *Superhero Instruction Manual* maintains no liability, implied or otherwise, concerning the consumer's final decision.

STEP 4: SECURE A SUPER HIDEOUT

Every superhero needs a secret lair to plan strategy and prepare to save the world.

It must be safe from evil-villain intruders.

STEP 5: CHOOSE YOUR SUPERPOWER

Superheroes don't just wake up one day with amazing powers.**

**Okay, okay. Sometimes a normal human gets a radioactive-spider bite and wakes up with super skills. But that's rare.

You must work hard to discover your inner BAM-BOOM-POW!

Underwater breathing?

ppfflt! gasp!
coughcoughcough

Supersonic speed?

vroom

swoosh

CRASH!

STEP 6: STORE UP SUPER ENERGY

Being super requires a LOT of power.
Be sure to mega-size breakfast . . .

and remember to stash a snack.

STEP 7: SAVE THE WORLD!

It's time to take action, hero!
Show the world what you're made of.

KA-BOOM!

CONGRATULATIONS!

You have now completed the seven steps to becoming a hero.

You should feel super!

. . . so be prepared. Sometimes the world needs saving two or three times before lunch.

There are all kinds of heroes.

But a true **SUPERhero** is always there when it counts.

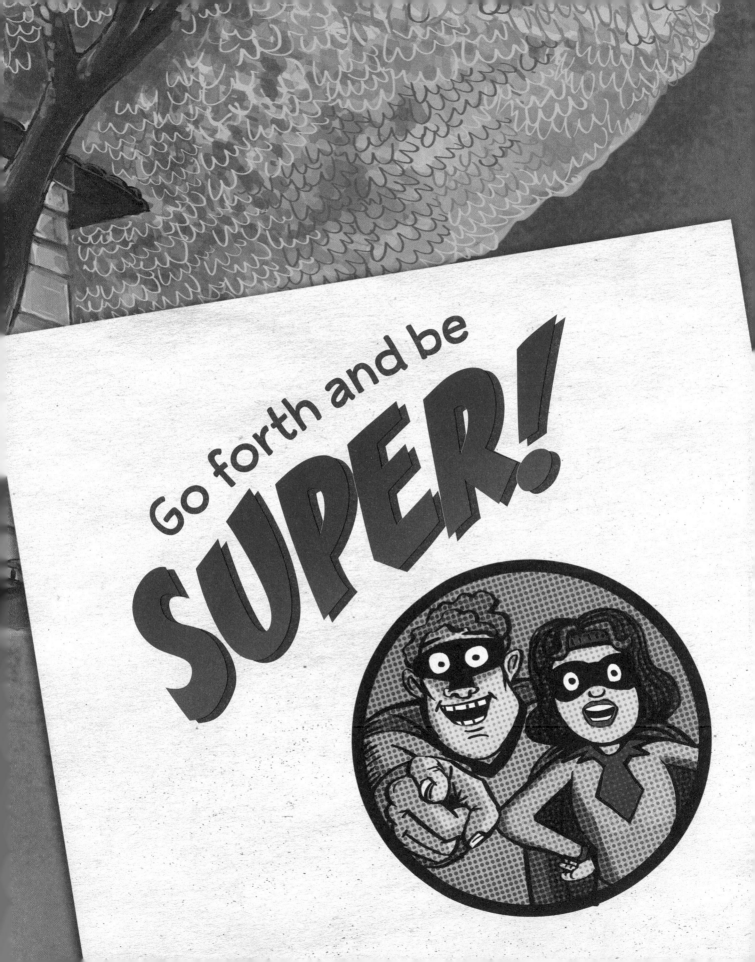

Kristy Dempsey

has held several secret identities through the years, but the most recent has her using her super-powers as a school librarian in Belo Horizonte, Brazil. Her previous picture books include *Me with You*, *A Dance Like Starlight*, and *Surfer Chick*, which received starred reviews as well as a National Parenting Publications Award.

Mark Fearing

has illustrated several books for children, including *The Book That Eats People* and *The Three Little Aliens and the Big Bad Robot*. His animated shorts have been seen on a variety of TV stations and at many film festivals, and he considers himself barely an adult. He currently works across mediums and loves to tell stories with words and pictures.